Mark Guy Pearse

Gold and Incense

a west country story

Mark Guy Pearse

Gold and Incense
a west country story

ISBN/EAN: 9783337237653

Printed in Europe, USA, Canada, Australia, Japan

Cover: Foto ©Andreas Hilbeck / pixelio.de

More available books at **www.hansebooks.com**

GOLD AND INCENSE

A West Country
Story · by MARK
GUY PEARSE

FORTY-SEVENTH
THOUSAND

LONDON
HORACE MARSHALL & SON

Dedication

TO SIDNEY HILL ESQ.
OF LANGFORD HOUSE
SOMERSET

It may add to the interest of my story if I state that it is perfectly true.

Chapter I

TO think it is Jennifer Petch of whom I am going to tell—little Jennifer. How she would laugh if she only knew of it, that shrill, silvery laugh of hers. It was her great gift. Jennifer was a philosopher in the matter of laughing; and philosophy is mostly a matter of knowing how to laugh and when.

And the village itself would wonder almost as

11

much as Jennifer herself, for very few of them could see anything to write about in her. Village people do not see much in what they see always, and Jennifer had lived among them all her days. There was a time when some of the younger folks thought they owed her a little bit of a grudge. For Sam Petch was the tallest, and straightest, and handsomest of the village lads; and the maidens who strolled down the lane on a summer's evening would go home with fluttering hearts and delicious dreams if Sam had chanced to come that way, as somehow he generally did; and if he had loitered laughing with them in the lane, as he never minded doing.

There was Phyllis, light of hair and blue of eye, light of step and light of heart, and light of hand, as her butter showed—not one of the lads had any chance with her so long as Sam was free.

There was Chloe, she of

the loose sun-bonnet, with gipsy face and gipsy eyes, who handled the rake so daintily, and drew the sweet hay together with such grace that nobody wondered if Sam Petch found it a great deal easier to turn his head that way than to turn it back again.

And on the Sunday night when the service was over, at the door of the little chapel, which was the village trysting place, there were half a dozen of the comeliest of the maidens, who found an excuse to linger talking, until Sam had gone his way.

It came on them all with an amazement of surprise,

especially as events of that kind were always busily whispered abroad at the slightest hint, and often without any hint at all—"Sam Petch was going to be married."

"Who to?" asked everybody, brightening with wonder.

After every likely lass had been guessed the voice fell, and the answer was given almost with a sense of wrong, "Why, to little Jennifer ! Whatever he can see in her I can't think."

For that matter, no more could Jennifer herself. Round and short of figure, red and brown of face, she

had never so much as ven-
tured to look at Sam, or to
think of him either. And
even now she was almost
sorry for him that she was
only plain little Jennifer,
and not like Phyllis or
Chloe.

And because the village
maidens could see no reason
for it in her looks they
concluded that there must
be some hidden wiliness,
.ome depth of craft for
which they were no match.
They talked it over as they
milked the cows, the white
stream falling with its
music into the pail. "She
knew what she was doing,
Jennifer did, a regular deep
one." It was told in the

lane with a laugh, as if each wanted to show that Sam was nothing to them, of course.

But the older folks talked of it differently. The women stood in the doorway of an evening with clusters of children about them, and according to them it was Sam who was the deep one. He knew what he was doing, did Sam. There were things, they said, and they spoke feelingly, that lasted longer than good looks and were worth more. And as the men came home with heavy steps from the day's work, with a smell about them like the smell of a field that the Lord hath blessed, they said that **a** little thrifty body like Jennifer was a prize for anybody to be proud of, and Sam Petch was a lucky fellow, that he was.

It was plain enough, whatever Jennifer thought—and she kept her thoughts mostly to herself—that Sam agreed with these older ones. He could not do enough to show his pride in Jennifer, and but that she refused all offers of finery, would have made his plain little sweetheart as gay as Phyllis or Chloe. Never an evening passed but you met them walking leisurely together, the declared sign of courtship, which was also known as "keeping company." It was thus distinguished from marriage, for which the accepted sign was that the wife kept three yards behind.

But when Sam and Jennifer were married they still went on "keeping company;" even though his long stride needed three of Jennifer's short steps, she was never behind, and Sam would have taken steps as short as hers before she should be. And if it be true that light hearts make easy travelling, they might well keep together, up hill and down. A glance was enough to show that things were flourishing with them. Their

19

cottage stood on the top of the hill, all set about with a garden fair, and at the side and back of the house grew "stuff" enough to send to market. Sam had rented a bit of a meadow where a couple of cows gave Jennifer the chance of showing her skill at clotted cream and butter. There, too, a troop of fowls had their run, and away in a corner three pigs added to the importance of Sam and to the cares of Jennifer. She, thrifty soul, made enough out of her department to pay the rent; up early, and always at work, her song only ceasing to make way for her silvery laugh. The older folks repeated their opinion now as a prophecy fulfilled, and took to themselves as much credit as if the prediction had been the chief cause of the prosperity.

Before three years had gone Jennifer's department was increased by the birth of two sturdy little sons. They were both the image of Sam, so the women declared; but the men saw in each the image of their mother, and counted it a pity that they were not girls, for the like of Jennifer they reckoned scarce.

Chapter II

IT was an evening toward the end of August, and the harvest was being gathered in. The fields on every side were dotted with the tented sheaves piled up as the custom is in the "catching" weather of the West, one sheaf reversed on the top of the cluster, so as to form a kind of roof. The long shadows of the shocks fell across the fields in the evening

22

light. All the country was
beautiful with that rich
restfulness which comes in
the autumn, as if the earth

had finished its work. The
glories of the sunset gave
the sky a hundred delicate
tints of gold and purple.

Here and there the wo-
men brought the sheaves,
whilst the men piled them
on the wagons. Away over
the hill country in the east
the great harvest moon was
rising.

Jennifer, busy as ever,
had got her two little ones
settled for the night, and
now was preparing a dainty
supper for Sam's return;
the savoury smell of it filled
the place.

Then it was that, as to
Job of old, one came breath-
less to the house with sad
tidings. Sam had slipped
from the stack and fallen
on his head.

" Is—he—dead ? " gasped
Jennifer.

26

No, he was not dead; but he had not spoken since his fall, and was quite unconscious. A messenger had been sent for the doctor, and the men were bringing Sam home, and would be here in a few minutes.

Up the hill came the group with the injured man in their midst, to all appearance dead. A great hush fell on the village as they passed slowly on, men in their shirt sleeves just as they had hurried in from the harvest field. The women and children stood at the doors with faces full of sympathy.

They bore him in at the little gate and through the

garden and up the stairs,
and laid him on the bed.

.   .   .   .   .

For weeks Sam lay on
his bed, whilst day and
night Jennifer waited on
him.

The neighbours stopped
the doctor to ask about him,
and the answer was ever
the same:

"He'll pull through; he'll
pull through," and the doctor tightened his mouth and
nodded his head; "but he
would have been a dead
man long ago if it had not
been for that brave little
wife of his."

Fracture of the skull and
concussion of the brain, and
a host of other ills, made

it a desperate fight with death. But Jennifer fought and won. Even in his unconsciousness Sam seemed to know the touch of her hand, and it soothed him; and the tone of her voice, and the moaning ceased.

But bit by bit their little fortune was swept away The savings of those three or four years were quickly spent; the cows had to be sold, and the meadow given up; the pigs and fowls were parted with.

The garden lay untended. And when, at last, the doctor had done with Sam, it was only to leave him an imbecile — helpless as a baby, and a great deal more troublesome — sometimes muttering to himself for hours together a round of unmeaning words; sometimes just crying all day long, and then again cross and peevish and perverse as any spoilt child.

The cottage was given up; they could not afford the rent of that.

Another was taken, the cheapest in all the village —one that was too bad for anybody else.

Half a crown a week and a loaf of bread from the parish was all that came in to supplement Jennifer's poor earnings of sixpence a day in the fields.

.   .   .   .   .

It was some few years after this had happened that I came to know Jennifer.

There she sat in the little chapel, her round and ruddy face without a wrinkle in it, all curves and dimples that were the settled homes of good humour and thankfulness; a face snugly surrounded by a black bonnet, set off with a clean white cap. Beside her were her two lads, their faces as clean and shining as plenty of soap and hard scrubbing could make them. You met her going home from the service, the short, round figure wrapped in a thick black shawl, trotting along with her hymn book in one

hand and a big umbrella
in the other, short and
round like herself. The
happy little lads went
bounding before her, the
three of them the very pic-
ture of gladness.

Yet it was almost wicked
of Jennifer to look so comfortable, when all the parish
knew that there was not a
poor body for miles around
that had so much trouble.
She certainly had no busi-
ness to be anything but the
most mournful and melan-
choly soul that ever went
grumbling along the high-
road, if you can measure
people's happiness by their
circumstances.

Follow her as she turns

down this narrow lane, skilfully picking her way in the mud. At the end of the lane is her cottage. One half of it has fallen, the cob-walls have given way, and the thatch hangs over the ruins. It was a wonder that what was standing did not follow, for there were cracks in the walls through which the wind whistled, and there were broken places in the roof through which the rain dripped.

But within was a greater sorrow than any that you could find outside. As Jennifer opens the door she hurries across the uneven floor to the rough settle by the fire. There is her husband—poor Sam!

As now she comes near and lays her hand upon his shoulder, the dull face is turned toward her with a smile. He tries to say something, but the mouth only opens without a word, and the tears fill his eyes. Jennifer bends and kisses him tenderly. "Poor dear," she says, as she gently strokes the hands that hold her own. "Poor dear, was he wanting us home again?"

Presently she slips the hand away so skilfully that her husband does not seem to know it, and takes off her bonnet and shawl.

The lads meanwhile have set the things for the Sunday dinner. It did not need much setting. On the rickety table was placed a knife —they had but one. There were three slices of bread, a thick round off the loaf, and on each slice a bit of cheese; "Double Gloucester" was, I think, the local name of it. The one big mug was filled from a large earthen pitcher.

Jennifer herself had set the kettle down by the wood fire, for if she had a weakness it was her cup of tea. But there was not much promise of any water boiling in a hurry; the tiny spark was almost lost in the big fireplace, a hearth opening into the chimney, and so constructed that a great deal more cold seemed to come down than heat went up.

The little family group stood and bent their heads in devout thanksgiving to the heavenly Father, and then the hungry lads fell to. As for Jennifer herself it seemed as if she never got her dinner at all. All her concern was to try and tempt her husband's appetite with a piece of bread and butter daintily cut ; and there was for him, too, a drop of milk. Yet even her hypocrisy could not manage to keep up her happy looks on nothing.

This was Sunday: a day indeed of rest and gladness. Other days she had to be up and about early to get the little lads their breakfast; and to make them ready for school; and to set her husband by the fire. Then she herself was off with the dawn, and sometimes before, to work all day in the fields. Her rough dress was stained earth colour from head to foot; a sack was tied round the skirts which were tucked well up out of the way. A big sun-bonnet protected her more often from the bleak winds and bitter rains than from the sun. From dawn till dusk she worked for six-pence a day; and then came home thanking God right heartily for the three shillings a week. And on that Jennifer managed to feed and clothe her household, and to pay the rent and to keep up her good looks.

The fact is, Jennifer was as we have said, a philosopher, and had made a great discovery. It was certainly worthy to be set alongside of the most famous inventions; and like many of them it had the one great defect—so few knew how to use it. Jennifer had little, it is true. She was, so to speak, but a moulting bird, half starved and shivering in the dreariest and dullest of cages—that is, if you looked at what *was*. But Jennifer found another world, in which she had a boundless freedom and strength, and here she went soaring like an eagle right up into the sun. It was what *wasn't* that she made so much of.

You pitied her, and spoke mournfully about her husband, as if he were a burden and worry. But Jennifer never seemed to hear it, and certainly could not see it.

"Poor dear," she said, "I can mind the day he asked me to be his wife. I did jump. And all the maidens in the parish would have liked him. When they heard about it they all went wondering whatever he could see in a poor little plain thing like me; but none of them wondered so much as I did. I never could do enough for him when he was well, and now that I have got my chance I should be ashamed if I did not make the best of it. Poor dear, he is as much to me as ever, and more too—husband and child all in one." And she said it over tenderly to herself, "Poor dear!"

But this was Jennifer s sentiment, and her sentiments were sacred and kept mostly for home use. It was the philosopher that met you more commonly. You spoke to her pitifully

of her husband's affliction,
and were almost startled at
the tone of her cheery voice.

" Yes, 'tis sad. But bless
you, think of what *might* ha'
been. If he was in racks
of torments all day long,
and me at his side doing
nothing else but poulticing
and trying to give him a bit
of ease ! Or if we was both
like he is—me and he, too,
a-setting by the fire and
never able to do anything
for each other, whatever
should us have done then ?
Only to think of it. And
there—it might ha' been ;
of course, it might ha' been.
What a mercy ! " And
Jennifer lifted up her hands.
" What a mercy ! "

You complained of the miserable cottage. But Jennifer was ready to point out its advantages, until the tumble-down place seemed to grow quite considerate and kindly.

"Well, you see it isn't half so bad as it *might* be. The cracks don't let the wind blow in where we do sit to. And the rain don't drip in where we do sleep to. *That* would be bad. And it *might* ha' done ; of course, it *might* ha' done. What a mercy!" And again Jennifer's hands were uplifted.

You began to pity her for the children's sake. But a

merry laugh cut that short
in a moment.

" Yes, I often think about
that," laughed Jennifer,
" *there might ha' been fourteen of them*. And, bless
you, whatever should I ha'
done if there had a-been
fourteen ! " And Jennifer
lifted up her hands and
laughed again, and then
slapped them down upon her
knees. "Fourteen of them !
Why, where should us all
have slept to ? And think
of the eating all round, and
the clothes and all. Fourteen ! And it *might* ha'
been. What a mercy ! "

You talked pathetically
about her work in the fields
—the dreariness of it and

the weariness, bending with
hoe from morning to night;
or kneeling at the weeds till
all the limbs ached.   But
Jennifer was
more than a

match for
you. "Ah,
that's it.
T h a t ' s
w h a t I
a l w a y s
say.   To think that it should
be such hard work and all
that, and that I should have
the strength for it. Now, if I
was one of them sort that is

always ailin' and failin', instead of being so strong as a horse! And I *might* ha' been ; of course, I *might* ha' been. What a mercy! Why, there's some as couldn't walk there and back, for 'tis sometimes three miles there and three miles back, and there's some as couldn't do it when they got there, for the weeds be terrible strong sometimes. And there's some as couldn't bear it, east wind and rain and snow. And I *might* ha' been one of them sort. What a mercy!"

This was Jennifer's philosophy.

Chapter III

NOW it chanced one day that the little village in which Jennifer lived was stirred by the ambition of the congregation to build a new chapel. The old place was not good enough; not even large enough. A great meeting was held, and the sluggish life of the place was quickened by a sermon from a stranger in the afternoon, followed by a public tea meeting. At night stirring speeches were

made and various promises
given. The well-to-do and
generous layman who acted
as the father of a group of
village chapels in the district would give fifty pounds.
One of the farmers would
cart the stones. Another
would give the lime. Others
made promises that ranged
down to a pound. There
the line was drawn. Those
who could do less than that
did not count.

Jennifer managed to get
to the meeting and sat
delighted at the promises of
one and another, neither
envying any nor even
wishing that she could do
some great thing.

"I will do what I can,"

49　　　D

she said, as she shook hands with the chairman at the close of the meeting.

"I am sure you will, Jennifer, your heart is good enough for anything," said he tenderly, thinking within himself how much the least gift would cost her.

The next day Jennifer was off to the fields, and as she hoed the lines of turnips she was talking to herself of the proposed new chapel.

"Silver it must be, I am afraid; but it isn't the colour for Him. I should like to give the Lord a bit of gold. If it isn't *that* it must be the biggest bit of silver there is."

Then Jennifer went on hoeing the weeds to the tune of the hymn that she hummed to herself :

" Kings shall fall down before Him,
    And gold and incense bring ;
All nations shall adore Him,
    His praise all people sing."

The tune rang out cheerily on the breeze as she went on, and the words got deeper down in her soul. For Jennifer boasted that she could sing. " If I can't do anything else I can sing," she said. There was very often a hymn on her lips and always one in her heart. She had her philosophy about singing. " I am not going to be beat

by the birds, and we are
nothing but a sort of creeping thing till we can sing.
What's the good of the blue
sky above us if we can't
fly up into it? And sing-
ing is wings to my think-
ing."

. . . .

Eight months had gone
by, and the time had come
for the opening of the new
chapel.

Then it was that Jennifer
came cautiously to her
friend and asked to speak
to him privately. They
went down the road to-
gether, and as soon as they
were past the houses of
the village she stopped and

took carefully from her pocket a little piece of paper which she put into his hands.

"There," she said, "that is for the new chapel."

He opened it and found a half sovereign. "I am so glad to give a bit of that colour, sir," and Jennifer's face beamed with joy.

But the good man started, quite frightened. "I cannot take it, Jennifer. Really I must not. Half a sovereign from you? No, it would not be right."

Jennifer pushed back his hand as he held it out to her. "Not take it!" she cried. "But you must take it, sir; 'tis the Lord's."

" But really you cannot afford it. It is very good of you."

"But I *have* afforded it, you see," she laughed; " and I am going to afford another before I have done."

He held the coin reluctantly in his hand. " It really hurts me to think of it; and you so poor as you are."

" Well, I am sorry to hurt anybody. But there's no need to be hurt about it a bit. I thought when I rang out that half sovereign that it was the prettiest music I ever heard, or shall hear till I get up among the angels. And they don't have a chance of anything like that,

I expect." And she laughed again.

"Well, Jennifer, I suppose I must take it," and he opened his collecting book to enter the subscription with her name, but she checked him instantly.

"No, sir, no. You must put it in the box. I did not mean to let anybody know, but I could not tell how to manage it. If I put it in the box my own self, why some of them might see me, and then I was afraid they might be after stopping my half a crown a week and my loaf of bread, thinking that I had come into a fortune all of a sudden." And she laughed again.

55

" No, Jennifer; we must have it down among the subscriptions, and it ought really to head the list. I will call it *Anonymous*, you know."

" Oh, that's much too fine a name for Jennifer Petch. Call it ' *Gold and Incense.*' I *do* know what that do mean, if anybody else don't," and Jennifer laughed again.

And so it was entered, and so it was duly announced. Jennifer blushed and laughed so much when it was read that any suspicious person might have found out her secret after all. But no one dreamed that this was Jennifer's assumed name.

It was not long before her good friend met with Jennifer again.

"I can't get over that half-sovereign of yours, Jennifer," he began. "I am really quite curious to know how you managed it. You will tell me, won't you?"

"Well, I s'pose I must," said Jennifer shyly; "but I meant to keep it all to myself, you know. Nobody knows about it but you."

"Well, then, I may know all, mayn't I?"

Little by little it all came out. And this was Jennifer's story:

"Well, it was the day

after the meeting that I
was singing to myself the
words,—

" Kings shall fall down before Him,
    And gold and incense bring,"

when it seemed to me like
as if I could see them
coming like Solomon in all
his glory, and laying down
their gifts at His dear feet ;
but, there, you will be
getting all my secret out
of me. It must come, I
s'pose. Well, the tune and
the words were sort of
ringing in my head when I
turned round out of the wind
for to—to—— You mustn't
be hard on me. It was to
take a *pinch of snuff.*"

  "Oh, Jennifer " !

"It was only a penn'orth a week, sir," she pleaded. "And it did seem to sharpen me up a bit out in the cold. Well, while I was taking it I laughed to myself. 'That's the nearest to *incense* that I can think of,' I said. 'I will give that to the Lord.' And, bless you, sir, would you believe it? I got to turning round out of the wind to make believe I had it, and it did every bit so well.

"The next Saturday, instead of giving the penny to a neighbour to get the snuff into market, I put the penny into an old broken teapot, and put it on top of the dresser, and I said, 'There's

a nest egg, then.' Well, I
quite longed for the next

Saturday to come, and then
there was a penny more.
And in three weeks there

was a threepenny bit. I
did think that was a prettier
colour for the Lord, but,
bless you, I liked the three
pennies better.

" That tiny little three-
penny bit in that great
teapot! I was most ready
to cry for it in there all by
its lonely little self. I
couldn't help thinking about
it till it came to be almost
like when I had to leave the
baby home and couldn't
think of anything else, and
thought I heard it a-crying
whenever so much as a
lamb would bleat or a
horniwink go crying over-
head.*

* A horniwink is in that dialect a
green plover or lapwing.

"My heart sort of went out to the poor little three-penny bit. 'You shall have company, my dear,' I said to myself, 'that you shall, before very long.'

"That night when I got home I was just going to get my cup o' tea, when it came to my mind, 'There's company for the poor little thing.' At first I tried to put away the thought, for I did dearly love my cup o' tea. Coming home tired and wet and cold, it was wonderful how it used to cheer and refresh a body. So I tried to think of something else. But the more I tried the more I couldn't. At last I sat down by the bit of fire and had it out with myself before I went to bed.

" ' You know,' I said to myself, 'a penny a week — what's that? Why, a whole year will only come to less than a crown piece. Gold and incense indeed, they are a long way off at that rate.' Then I got down the broken teapot and looked in. I had to turn it round and round before I could so much as see it. And when I did I was fair ashamed of myself. 'Poor little thing,' I said, ' and to think that you must wait three weeks for company! No, you shan't.'

" Well, I put it back

again and then screwed up my courage to see what I could make believe for tea. At last I thought I would toast some crusties till they were nice and brown. Then I would pour the boiling water on them 'The colour will be right enough,' I said, 'but what about the taste, I wonder? However, taste as they mind to, there's threepence a week!' So I went to bed, and that night I dreamed that the broken teapot was so full of sovereigns that I was quite frightened and woke all of a tremble.

"I dare say it didn't taste exactly right at the first going off. But very soon I came to like it just as well. And I really do believe, after all said and done, 'tis more strengthener and more nourishinger than the tea.

"So the next Saturday, instead of asking a neighbour to bring home an ounce of tea, I put the threepenny bit in the broken teapot. And there was fourpence a week. And I changed it into a shilling; and then it grew into a half-crown; and last of all it came to *half a sovereign*.

"I was glad to have a bit of that colour. It was years since I had so much as seen one of them. 'Tis the only colour that is good enough for Him. And I haven't done yet, please God. In eight months' time there will be another, and that will make a whole sovereign. It isn't like doing the thing at all to do it by halves. That is what I have set my heart upon. That will be ' *Gold and Incense—One Pound.*' "

Chapter IV

FOR days after hearing
it her good friend could
think of nothing but Jennifer's story. His own gifts
to the new chapel and that
of the others seemed poor
and little beside her offering
—it was the mite which
was more than they all had
given. He felt that he
could not rest until he had
found for her something
better than the ill-paid toil
in the fields. As he rode

on his way he chanced to
see a notice announcing
the sale of a coppice of
some twenty acres, freehold.
Here was the opportunity
of serving
Jennifer, and
at once he
made haste

to avail himself of it. The bit of ground was bought, coppice and all. Then he made his way to her house.

It was seldom that any one passed her cottage, and when he saw it he was distressed and ashamed that he had not done anything for her before.

Jennifer had just got home, tired and wet and cold. He came into the cheerless place and sat down.

"I had no idea that your cottage was in such a wretched state, Jennifer; I wonder you could live in it," he began.

"Well, 'tis wonderful

how comfortable we do get on in it, sir." And Jennifer spoke as cheerfully as ever. "I s'pose if it was better we should have to pay more, so we must set one thing against another, you know."

"Well, I am going to build you another—a new one; I have made up my mind to that. And look. Jennifer, you shall have it for your own as soon as I can get it up, and you can pay me for it."

"I daresay, sir," laughed Jennifer, and she wondered that her friend could seem to joke on such a subject.

"But I mean it," said he, "and, of course, I am going

to put you in the way to
do it."

"Thank you, sir," said
Jennifer, quite unable to
see any meaning in the
promise. "You see, there's
the Guardians, what will
they say and all if I do
go living in a fine new
house?"

"The Guardians! Oh, you
must go and tell them that
you don't want any more
of their money or their loaf
either."

"But, sir," said Jennifer,
trying to laugh, yet almost
too bewildered to succeed,
"half crowns and loaves
of bread won't grow out of
a new house any more than
an old one, you know."

" Well, Jennifer, that is what I have come to see you about. Your boys are growing up quite big lads now. What are you going to do with them? What are they — twelve or thirteen years old at least ? "

" Just about, sir. I have given them so much head learning as I can. I suppose they must be going out for to do something; but there, 'tis terrible hard for to think about their going away."

" Oh, but I don't think they need go away, Jennifer. I have come to tell you that I have bought that piece of coppice over there. Now, what I have

been thinking is this. You
and your boys can cut it
all down, and make up the
faggots with the under-
wood, and sell it for what
it will fetch. That shall
go toward the new cottage.
And when the land is
cleared I will let it to you,
and the boys can turn it
into potato ground."

Poor Jennifer sat down
without a word. She could
not take it all in so sud-
denly and it bewildered
her. Clinging to the old
ways of her life, and satis-
fied with the simple round,
she shrank from so large
a venture, involving so
many changes.

" Well, what do you

say?" asked her friend, somewhat disappointed that she did not see all the advantages which were so plain to him.

"I don't know what to say, sir. 'Tis very kind of you. But——"

"But what, Jennifer?"

"I was going to say, if you don't mind, I should like one day more in the fields to think it all over. 'Tis a wonderful place for thinking about anything. And nobody but the heavenly Father to talk to."

"Yes, Jennifer, take a day by all means." And he rose to go. "Only remember that you will make out of the coppice more in

a month than you can
make in the fields in a
year; and be your own
mistress, too, and come and
go as you like."

"In a month!" she said
gravely. "Then I am
afraid I should be putting
my heart in the broken
teapot, instead of my
money."

However, the next day's
thought in the fields showed
her a hundred advantages
for the boys in the pro-
posal, whatever it might
mean for her husband and
herself. And the cottage,
too; the very suggestion
of a new one seemed to
make the cracks bigger
and the leaks worse.

Something would have to be done if she stayed there. So it was settled, yet not without a sigh. This was to be her farewell of the fields.

The sun was setting as she took up her hoe and turned homeward. At the gate she stayed a minute or two, as if to say good-bye. To her eyes the scene was almost sacred. There were the fields with all the young growth of the early spring, and beyond this was the rough outline of the hedges where the rabbits played. There were the hills where the brown trees reached up to the firs, and from beyond which

there often came the roar
of the ground swell when
the great Atlantic breakers
thundered on the shore.
The very birds had been
her company and friends,
and she loved them every
one — the lark that went
soaring upward with an
evening hymn; the thrush
and the blackbird that
piped from the tree top;
the rooks that went slowly
homeward, a very cloud in
the sky, all had come as
if to solace and gladden
her, and she blessed them
all. Her heart went out
in thanks to God, as the
memory of a thousand
mercies rose within her.
She took the old worn mit-

tens from her rough, red hands with a sigh, and shut the gate as if she were shutting that chapter of her life.

Chapter V

BUT Jennifer found that it was more than a new chapter in her life— it was a new world into which she stepped at once: a world where everything was so much more than she ever dared to ask or think, that half the time she was like one in a dream, and shook herself, as she said, to see if she were really awake. Before she could get to her door,

the lads came rushing out
to meet her with the news
that a pair of leggings had
come for each of them,
and a couple of billhooks;
and there in all their pride
they stood, ready to go
forth at once and cut down
all the forests of the world,
if they had but the chance.
And they must needs take
their mother, hungry and
tired as she was, away to
the edge of the coppice, to
show her the place that
was cleared for their new
cottage. Poor Jennifer sigh-
ed a prayer that the Lord
would keep her humble;
worthy of it all she felt
she never could be.

At dawn the next day

the boys were up—men in
the estimate of themselves,
and more than most men
in their eagerness to get
at the work, sweetened as
the thought of it was by
the fact that every stroke
was to make the coming
cottage their own. Break-
fast to-day was a duty
somewhat begrudged. They
were impatient of its delay
At last they were off and
at it, coat and waistcoat
flung aside.

An old labourer had been
sent on that first day to
direct them in the work,
for there are two ways even
of cutting down a coppice
—a right and a wrong
—and of tying faggots.

But he got there only to find a good half-day's work had somehow already been got through.

But Jennifer herself never did so little. To her it was all so new and strange that she could scarcely steady herself to do anything. In place of the silent fields there came the cheery voices of her lads, and the hacking of the billhook; then the bending of the tough boughs was new to her, and the binding of the faggots.

And underneath all was a certain glow of gladness that disturbed her. She was so near home, and was now her own mistress too, that she could not resist the temptation of going off to look after her " poor dear," as she called her husband.

And instead of hurrying back, she stayed to wrap him up, and then must needs bring him out along the lane and over the thick bed of dead leaves and through the rough under-growth of the coppice to sit on the first faggot that she had bound. And there she sat beside him, while the sun peeped in at them between the young leaves; and the bold robin hopped up to look at them in won-der; and all the birds sang to them, and the sweet breath of things came with its benediction. Presently, as if ashamed of herself, she hurried off to join the busy sons. Yet before long there was Jennifer,—the hardest-working woman in the parish at other times— creeping slyly over to have

a cheery word with her husband, and trying to amuse him by her skill in this craft, until her happy laughter rang out upon the silence, and even he tried to join. In a day or two, however, both mother and sons had got into the mysteries of the art; and went on steadily clearing the place, amazing themselves and everybody else at the speed with which the work was done. No hour seemed too early to begin, and none too late to leave off.

Soon there arrived the man who had bought the wood and faggots, and then began the further mystery of accounts, each faggot duly entered and each payment recorded. And Jennifer's pride found a new subject in the cleverness of her sons, for the minutest matters seemed to require the two heads to settle it.

But now it was that there came Jennifer's great trouble. Such joy could not fail to bring with it some bitterness somewhere.

Three pounds an acre was the price to be given for the clearing. And twenty acres came to nothing less than *sixty pounds*.

To Jennifer, who had not seen a bit of gold for years until she had given the half sovereign to the new chapel, it was really a terrible thing to have to do with so much money. The little broken teapot looked full, and the top of the dresser was no safe place in which to keep such treasures. She could not sleep at night, but must needs get up and go fumbling about to feel if it was all right. She dreaded to leave home, and went back three or four times to see to her husband, she said; but even he had to wait until she had looked at the teapot. The little that she spent upon the household was a mere nothing. She feared to carry so much all at once to her good friend to whom it was to be paid toward the new cottage. At last the lads were sent off to him with a message entreating him to come as soon as possible. " I shall go out of my mind or into the 'sylum," Jennifer declared, and began to wish once more for the sweet simplicity of the fields and her sixpence a day. However, that trouble was soon done with, and time, the kindly healer of our griefs, made even this tolerable.

The work was by no means done when the coppice was cleared. Roots and stumps had to be dug up, and the ground to be cleared for planting the potatoes, and the seed had

to be bought ; in all of
which her good friend took
as much interest as if it
was his own, and more.

And here was a new lot
of accounts to be duly recorded. Jennifer was glad
to leave all that to her

boys, who sat every even-
ing figuring away until it
seemed to her, as she looked over their shoulders,
that they did more busi-
ness than all the rest of
the world put together.

Chapter VI

IT was five or six years afterwards that I saw Jennifer again. At that time the coppice and cottage were her own freehold. The cottage was covered with creepers: the little garden was full of fruit trees and flowers. A row of beehives was ranged across one side of it. At the back there strutted and clucked a great host of fowls. Farther away a

dozen pigs lay in their
sties, and grunted their
satisfaction with the best
possible of worlds.

The potato ground was
wonderful; no such pota-
toes grew anywhere else.
The soil, enriched by the
decay of the woods for

years, yielded prolifically, and the first potatoes of the district that came to the market were Mrs. Petch's, as they called her now. But Mrs. Petch herself was just the same dear old Jennifer, as simple as of old. Her husband had passed away; without pain he had sunk to rest. The lads were big, broad-shouldered fellows who walked beside their little mother with more pride of her than ever.

At every collection now there is a bit of gold from somebody, and if it ever has to be announced, it still is read out, "Gold and Incense." But even gold has lost something of its charm to Jennifer, and on special occasions she whispers, "No other colour is good enough for Him, except it is a five-pound note."

But there is one matter in which Jennifer sticks to her opinion and will yield to nobody.

"You may say what you mind to, after all said and done, crusties is more nourishinger and strengthener than tea. I've a-tried both, and do know *that*."

THE END.

Butler & Tanner, Frome and London.

www.ingramcontent.com/pod-product-compliance
Lightning Source LLC
Chambersburg PA
CBHW020032030726
47499CB00007B/2381